I0759639

CUENTO DE LUZ

To my friend Carmen, the violinist.
Thanks for your wisdom and friendship.
—Nívola Uyá

This book is printed on **Stone Paper** that is **Silver Cradle to Cradle Certified®**.

Cradle to Cradle™ is one of the most demanding ecological certification systems, awarded to products that have been conceived and designed in an ecologically intelligent way.

Cuento de Luz™ became a **Certified B Corporation** in 2015. The prestigious certification is awarded to companies that use the power of business to solve social and environmental problems and meet higher standards of social and environmental performance, transparency, and accountability.

The illustrations in this book have been made with mixed techniques, watercolor, acrylics, pencil, and botanical printing.

Thank you, Gaspar, for opening the doors of your fascinating world to us.
The creation of this work has received support from the Institut d'Estudis Baleàrics.

institut d'estudis baleàrics

he Soul of the Violin
Text and illustrations © 2024 by Nívola Uyá
© 2024 Cuento de Luz SL
Poniente 92 | Pozuelo de Alarcón | 28223 | Madrid | Spain
www.cuentodeluz.com
Original title in Spanish: *El alma del violín*
English translation by Jon Brokenbrow
ISBN: 978-84-19464-70-5
1st printing, Legal Deposit Spain: M-4943-2024
Printed in PRC by Shanghai Cheng Printing Company, May 2024, print number 1922-13

The Soul of the Violin

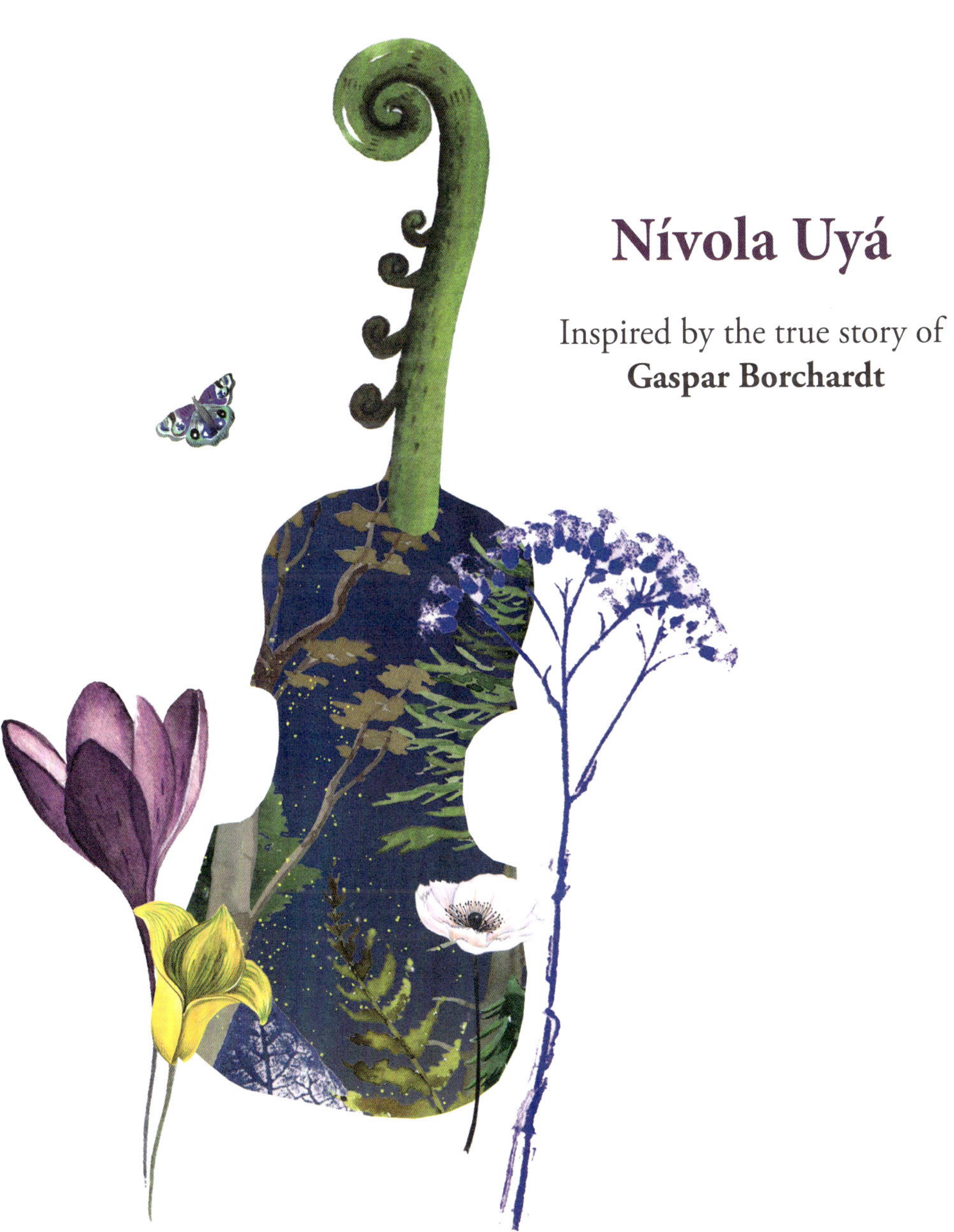

Nívola Uyá

Inspired by the true story of
Gaspar Borchardt

Gaspar was a sensitive, inquisitive little boy who grew up in Germany surrounded by wonderful sounds.

The melody of his childhood echoed the sounds of the forest.

He dreamed of being a great collector of sounds and developed a finely tuned ear. He became a skilled craftsman.

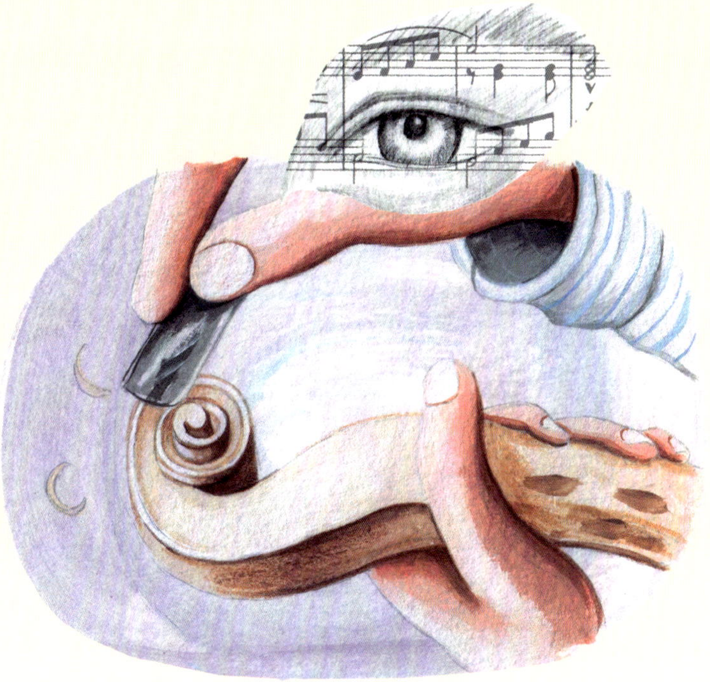

Gaspar has dedicated his life to transforming wood
into precious instruments with his hands.

And violinists, conductors, and collectors all agree that this brilliant luthier, an instrument maker, is a true virtuoso.

As his experience grew, so did his dream.

“I want to make the best violin in the world, as perfect as a Stradivarius,” he told himself again and again, determined to create the perfect instrument.

A unique violin needs extraordinary wood. He decided to make it out of flame maple, a tree famous for its strikingly colored timber. By chance, before setting off to find it, he met a remarkable violinist.

"I'll play that violin," Janine Jansen told him.

Gaspar set off for Bosnia, where there were still forests as old as the tree of his dreams.

The trip wasn't easy. He had to deal with a foreign language, forests that still contained dangerous mines left over from a war, and illegal logging.

On the way, lots of people helped guide him, telling him stories that ranged from surprising to absolutely magical.

Walking along a hillside, searching for the flame maple, he met an **eagle**.

“I’m looking for the ‘mother tree’ of the forest,” said Gaspar to the eagle. “The one that loves and cares for all its children, elders, and sick neighbors. Its music will embrace us. Have you seen it around here?”

“Perhaps,” replied the eagle without looking back, and flapped away over the trees.

As he walked through the meadows in the valley, he crossed paths with the **north wind**.

“Have you seen the maple who sweeps up the cool morning dew in its leaves every day? Who can greet the sunrise as beautifully as **Elgar’s ‘Chanson de Matin’**?” he asked, inspired.

The wind danced around him and, whistling gently, continued on its way.

Suddenly, a **goat** appeared, leaping between the ferns.

"I'm looking for the old maple, the guardian of time who fills us with energy and a love of life, just like **Vivaldi's *Four Seasons***. Have you seen it around here?" asked Gaspar, beginning to feel more than a little impatient.

The goat listened to him and then skipped off, muttering that a summer storm was on the way.

As Gaspar walked along the path through the ancient forest, **rain** started to fall.

“Listen to me,” he said. “You may be friends with a tree that’s seen a whole lot of storms. I’m looking for it. It’s the only one capable of transmitting all the emotions of the thunder and lightning in **Beethoven’s Sixth Symphony**.”

Just then, a bolt of lightning streaked across the sky, and rain fell harder than ever. Almost as quickly, the rain stopped, leaving behind a light mist.

He walked deeper into the green forest and met a **brown bear**. Now feeling quite discouraged, he asked the bear:

"Do you know the tree with wood like flames, whose fibers are capable of transmitting the deepest of emotions?"

"Perhaps," said the bear nonchalantly.

"Please, try and remember. I'm sure you've sat beneath it and felt the murmuring of the forest and the sound of nature when it's hurt, like in **Wagner's opera *Siegfried*.**"

But when he looked up, the bear had disappeared among the spruces.

Next to a mountain lake, a **herd of deer** grazed. Gaspar walked over to them, feeling quite exasperated.

"Can you tell me which way to go to find the tree that listens to the stories of the meadow flowers and the forest animals, just like in **Mahler's Third Symphony**?"

One deer trotted over to him.

"Amazing things happen in the forests," he said. "You can find that special tree you're talking about in the place where nature blooms." He pointed north with his antlers.

"That sounds to me just like the ballet from **Stravinsky's *Rite of Spring***!" cried Gaspar, feeling his enthusiasm flooding back.

At last! In the very heart of the mountainous forest, among the soaring beech and spruce trees, there stood an ancient flame maple, hundreds of years old. Gaspar could hear its resonance and smelled it with his eyes closed. It was absolutely perfect.

But as he stroked its trunk, letting his fingertips explore the grooves in its bark, he said to himself:

“I can’t just chop down such a magnificent tree. There can only be a few like it left.”

After making his magical discovery, Gaspar returned to his workshop in Cremona, Italy. His dream of crafting the perfect violin had faded away.

He carried on with his normal routine: a delicate universe of beautiful, precise details swirled back into action in his workshop.

One year after discovering the "mother tree," he received some surprising news. Another great tree had been cut down during an operation to clear away the land mines.

Gaspar jumped into his car and drove for hours, crossing into the Balkan peninsula until he reached the beautiful forest where the trunk of a magnificent flame maple lay on the ground.

As he stroked the wood and tapped it with his fingers, the trunk reverberated with the echo of the sap that had once coursed through it. He could still feel its presence.

"As beautiful as it looks, it'll sound even better!" said the craftsman as he felt how the symphony of the tree filled the air and made time stand still.
"I'll pour my soul into this instrument!"

This book was inspired by the documentary *The Quest for Tonewood,* the story of Gaspar Borchardt, a luthier, or someone who makes string instruments, as he faces the greatest challenge of his life: crafting the perfect violin.

The adventure chronicles the pursuit for the mystic flame maple, a tree found only in the ancient forests of the Balkans, a region in southeastern Europe.

The fascinating documentary transmits a love of nature and our connection with it, at the same time exploring the passion and innocence that mark the first steps in the creative process.

This film encouraged me to contact the violin maker with the idea of turning his wonderful experience into a picture book.

One year later, I traveled together with my daughter from Spain to visit his beautiful workshop in the Piazza del Duomo in Cremona, Italy. He introduced us to the stages involved in making a violin, and we were able to closely observe the expert process that combines mind, heart, and hands.

All of these experiences and emotions resulted in the creation of *The Soul of the Violin.*

The pieces of music dotted throughout this story were selected with Carmen González, a violinist from the Acordes School of Music. All of them express a great passion for nature.

"Chanson de Matin" by Edward Elgar

The Four Seasons by Antonio Vivaldi

The Sixth Symphony by Ludwig van Beethoven

Siegfried by Richard Wagner

The Third Symphony by Gustav Mahler

The Rite of Spring by Igor Stravinsky